AMOS and SUSIE
an Amish story

by Merle Good
illustrated by Cheryl Benner

Illustrations by Cheryl Benner
Design by Cheryl Benner and Dawn J. Ranck
Amos and Susie
Copyright ©1993 by Good Books, Intercourse, PA 17534
International Standard Book Number: 0-934672-46-6
    (paperback)
International Standard Book Number: 1-56148-088-6
    (hardcover)
Library of Congress Catalog Card Number: 93-11483

Library of Congress Cataloging-in-Publication Data
Good, Merle.
    Amos and Susie : an Amish story / by Merle Good :
illustrated by Cheryl Benner.
        p. cm.
    Summary: Rhyming text follows two Amish children through
the four seasons as they ice skate on a frozen winter pond, can
peaches in summer, and pursue other activities.
    ISBN 1-56148-088-6 (hardcover) : $12.95. — ISBN
0-934672-46-6 (pbk.) : $4.95
    [1. Amish—Fiction. 2. Seasons—Fiction. 3. Stories in rhyme.]
I. Benner, Cheryl A., 1962- ill. II. Title.
Pz8.3.G588Am   1993
[E]—dc20   93-11483
                                                 CIP AC

Good Books
Intercourse, PA 17534

They hurried home, and grabbed their skates
when all their chores were done,
And Amos always tried to race,
but Susie usually won.

While mothers quilted overhead
a roof above their play,
The girls pretended secret worlds
and shared a whispered day.

When Uncle Benny's big barn burned,
  it was a sad surprise,
But everyone helped clean it up
  and watched the rafters rise.

The fun of planting rows of peas
across the garden patch
Was beating Susie to the end—
but she was hard to catch.

The picnic meant the end of school,
and all the parents came.
The "scholars" played against their dads
and won the baseball game.

The first that Susie got to hold
    her cousin, Sarah Anne,
The baby cried and sniffed—then smiled—
    as only babies can.

"The threshing gives me itchy sweat,"
    said Amos to his Pop.
"Be thankful for the harvest, son;
    the sweat is worth the crop."

They all pitched in on canning day,
  and Susie helped along.
The jars filled up with "winter food,"
  and each pinged out a song.

They loved when Grandma's birthday came;
they knew what they would take,
Surprising Grandma with a treat
of homemade ice cream cake.

When Amos saw the newborn calf,
he scurried up the hill.
"I get to choose the name," he yelled,
"let's call her Daffodil!"

On sister Rachel's wedding day,
    they prayed and sang and ate
And peeked at tables heaped with gifts
    and got to stay up late.

The Christmas program at the school
made Amos worry some.
He gave his poem perfectly,
delighting Pop and Mom.

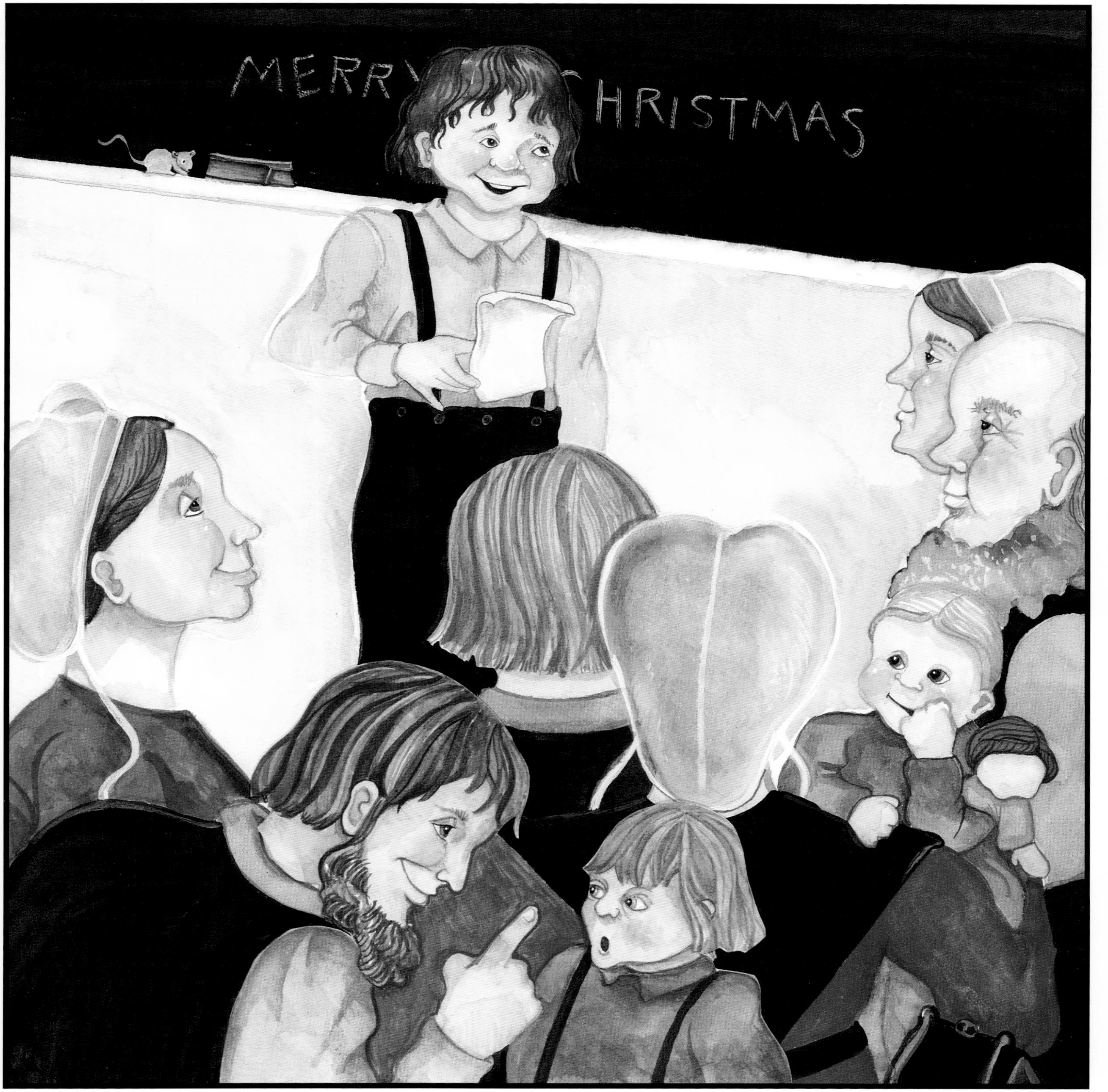
MERRY CHRISTMAS

January

There are about 135,000 Old Order Amish adults and children (all in North America). They live in 22 states and one Canadian province; 75% live in Ohio, Pennsylvania, and Indiana. Playing games and having fun, such as ice skating, is commonplace.

February

Many Amish women and girls like to make quilts. The old quilts, often made from leftover scraps, are famous for their solid colors. For some Amish families today, quiltmaking provides extra income.

March

Yes, barnraisings do still happen. Within days of a fire, neighbors and relatives gather to clean up the remains of the fire. Then on a given day, many dozens turn out, often including some non-Amish persons, to raise a new barn.

April

The Amish believe in taking good care of the earth. Farming is the preferred vocation. Gardens are usually large and well tended.

May

Most Amish children attend one-room or two-room schools, administered by a local Amish committee. The U.S. Supreme Court granted the Amish the right to complete only eight grades of formal schooling. The Amish believe wisdom is more important than excess information.

June

Children have a special place in the Amish world. From the moment of birth until the time of death, an Amish individual is surrounded by a network of family, church, and community.

July

Work is part of life for the Amish. It is not drudgery; it's an opportunity to be helpful. Harvest is a happy time, a natural part of life's cycles.

August

Preserving and canning food is commonplace. The abundance of food on winter shelves guarantees good eating all year round.

September

"Visiting" remains a highlight of Amish life. In a world with no telephone, television, radios, or cars, the pace of life is slower. And visiting others face to face becomes the main facet of social life.

October

Autumn signals the end of the growing season. It's time to gather in the crops. It can also be a time for new life. Most Amish children learn a great deal about animals.

November

An Amish wedding marks a high point in the life of the community. The all-day affair begins with a lengthy church service which includes the wedding itself. A wedding feast is served at noon. Hundreds of guests come for all or part of the day, which ends in singings. Gifts are generally practical.

December

Christmas is a religious holiday for the Amish. They express caution about the extravagant commercialization in larger society. It's a time to celebrate faith, family, friendship, and good food. Gifts are small and practical.

About the Author

Merle Good has written numerous books and articles about the Amish, including the beautiful book *Who Are the Amish?* and the popular children's book *Reuben and the Fire.* In addition to The People's Place, he and his wife Phyllis oversee a series of projects in publishing and the arts. They live in Lancaster, PA with their two daughters.

About the Artist

Cheryl Benner is an artist and designer who lives near Lancaster, PA with her husband Lamar and sons Austin and Grant. She is illustrator of two other children's books, *The Boy and the Quilt* and *Applesauce.*

She is co-author and designer with Rachel Thomas Pellman of a series of Country Quilt Pattern books, as well as *Favorite Applique Patterns, Volumes 1-6.*

For more information about the Amish, write to or visit The People's Place, P. O. Box 419 (Route 340), Intercourse, PA 17534, an Amish and Mennonite heritage center (of which Merle Good and his wife Phyllis are Executive Directors). Or request a free list of books about the Amish.